W9-BSC-090

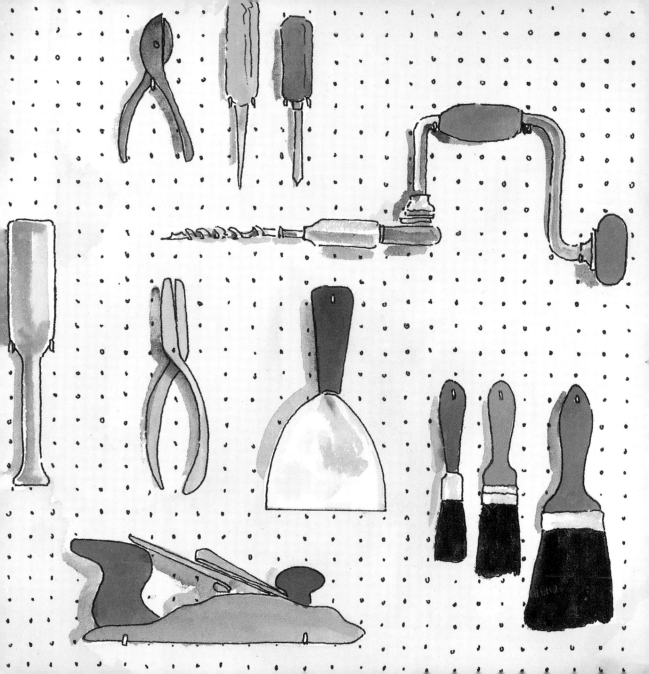

The Grandpa Days

by Joan W. Blos
illustrated by Emily Arnold McCully

SIMON AND SCHUSTER BOOKS FOR YOUNG READERS

Published by Simon & Schuster Inc., New York

![logo]

SIMON AND SCHUSTER BOOKS FOR YOUNG READERS
Simon & Schuster Building, Rockefeller Center,
1230 Avenue of the Americas, New York, New York 10020.

Text copyright © 1989 by Joan W. Blos
Illustrations copyright © 1989 by Emily Arnold McCully
SIMON AND SCHUSTER BOOKS FOR YOUNG READERS
is a trademark of Simon & Schuster Inc.
Manufactured in the United States of America

10 9 8 7 6 5 4 3 2 1

Library of Congress Cataloging-in-Publication Data

Blos, Joan W.   The grandpa days.
   SUMMARY: Philip comes up with just the right project
to build with Grandpa during their week together, but first
he has to learn the difference between wishes
and good planning.
   [1. Grandfathers—Fiction.]   I. McCully, Emily Arnold, ill.   Title.
PZ7.B6237Gr   1989   88-19801
ISBN 0-671-64640-0

When Philip visited his grandpa for a week, his grandpa told him how he'd built a tree house for Philip's mama when she was his little girl.

He showed him the special drawings he had made,
and explained to Philip how they helped to make
the house just right.

So Philip made some special drawings too.
He rolled them up and took them to his grandpa
to show what he wanted to make.

Philip's grandpa looked at Philip's drawings.
Then he looked at Philip.

"Philip," he began, "to make a rocket ship like that you'd have to have many people, and many special machines. Here there are just the two of us and my old carpenter's tools."

Then Philip's grandpa showed him all the tools,

the hammer,

the plane,

the screwdriver,

and the brace-and-bit.

He showed him how to use each one,
and then he gave Philip a turn.

The next day Philip made some other drawings.
He rolled them up and took them to his grandpa
to show what he wanted to make.

Philip's grandpa looked at the new drawings.
Then he looked at Philip.

"Philip," he began, "a racing car like that needs many metal parts. It needs tires made of rubber and windows made of glass. Here we have wood of different shapes and kinds, but it is always wood."

And Philip's grandpa showed him the one-by-ones and
two-by-fours, the planks and quarter-rounds.
He told him the names of the trees from which they came:
pine and oak and mahogany, and maple and ash and birch.

Before he made another drawing,
Philip thought hard and long.

He thought of the tools his grandpa had
and the different kinds of wood.
He thought of the things his grandpa knew
that he would have to learn.

And he thought of a new idea.

When the plans were done he rolled them up
and showed them to his grandpa.

"Philip, let's get going!" said his grandpa.
"We've got work to do!"

They worked all that day and the next,
the two of them together. They sawed and planed
and hammered and sanded,

and hammered and painted and drilled.

They were glad when the sky turned blustery,
and snow began to fall.

Next day, when Philip's mama came,
everyone wanted to try the sled.

But Philip rode it first.

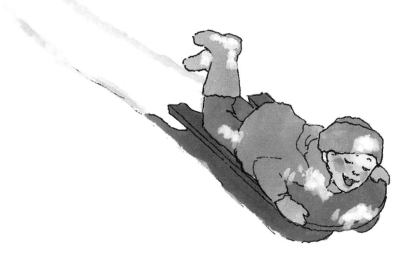

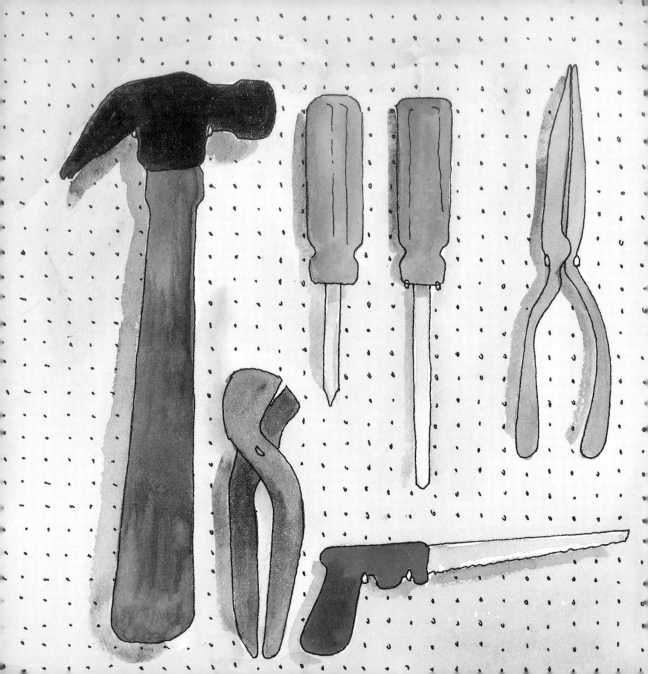

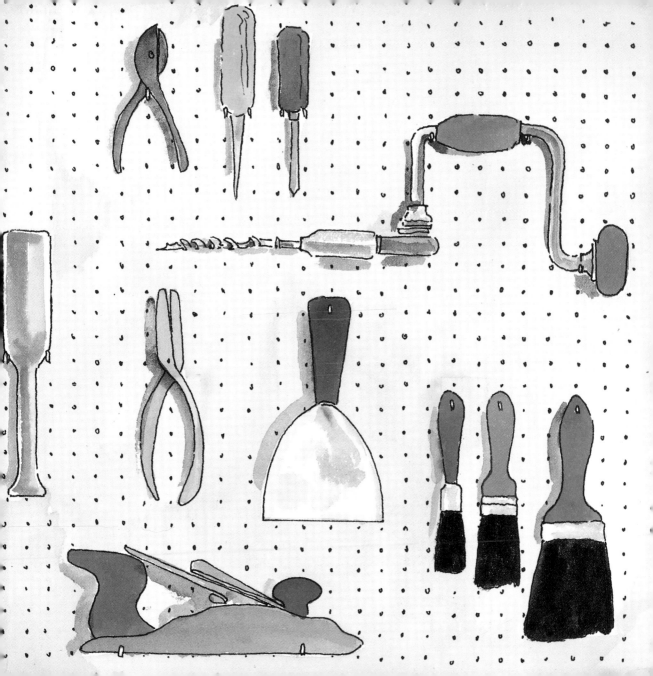

DATE DUE

AG 08 '93 / MR 18 '97		
OC 14 '93 / SE 24 '97		
FE 28 '94 / DE 26 '00		
MR 18 '94 / AP 19 '01		
JY 06 '94 / AG 01 '01		
DE 22 '94		
MY 02 '95		
JE 14 '95		
NO 28 '95		
AP 02 '96		
JE 16 '96		
MR 04 '97		